Other children's books by Storytellers Ink include:

Beautiful Joe

Black Beauty

Kitty the Raccoon

The Pacing Mustang

Lobo the Wolf

If a Seahorse Wore a Saddle

The Lost & Found Puppy

The Living Mountain

Sandy of Laguna

Father Goose & His Goslings

Cousin Charlie the Crow

William's Story

By Debra Duel

Illustrated By Donna Ryan

Published by Storytellers Ink
Seattle, Washington

ISBN 1-880812-02-9

Printed in the United States of America

William flicked his tail steadily and stared at the strangers as they lifted the sofa and carried it out of the apartment.

He followed the men and the sofa out of the building, up a metal ramp and into a long, dark truck. There he stood on his hind legs and pushed his white chin against the stuffed panda bear that was poking out of the wooden toy chest. His whiskers twitched. The scent of his friend, Sarah, filled his nostrils. He closed his eyes.

Suddenly, the floor of the truck shook and the pounding footsteps coming up the metal ramp echoed. William darted past the men. He ran to a shrub and sat under it, watching the strangers load Sarah's belongings into the truck. Soon the apartment was empty, and the men pulled the ramp into the truck, closed the doors and drove away.

"Sorry, William. The management at our new place said absolutely no pets," said Sarah's mother. "That means Sarah can't feed the neighborhood strays. You'll be okay—you're one tough cat." Sarah's mother bent down and scratched William between his ears. Then she got into her car and left.

William sat there waiting for the familiar sound that would tell him dinner was on the way. He stretched out in the sun and listened for Sarah. He closed his eyes and pulsed the tip of his tail.

Before long William heard the school bus pull into the lot. He got up with a start and ran to the usual stop. The familiar crowd of boys and girls bolted down the walkway, but Sarah was not with them.

Even so, William was eager to get inside Sarah's building. It was time to eat. He pulled a fast trick—he slid inside the double glass doors with the children and hurried down the hall. Then he stopped and stared at Sarah's door. It was a dark wooden door that was no different from the others that lined the dimly lit corridor, but William managed to meow in front of the right address every time.

Dinner couldn't be far away. The door would open soon, and William would point his scarred nose in the air and brush up against Sarah's denim covered legs. She would set the dish down just inside the apartment's doorway, and William would clean the plate.

William gave a soft meow and then cried out a little louder. "Meow!"

"Scat!" shouted an angry voice. William turned and saw a huge woman flapping a dripping dish rag toward him. "Go away, you miserable ol' tom. Cats aren't allowed to roam the halls in this building. The manager's going to hear about you!" William's pink pads barely met the carpeting as he flew down the hall to escape the towel. But after a minute or two, he trotted back to the door. It was nearly dark; his dinner was late and he was hungry.

William stared at the apartment door. He scratched at it. He meowed. Nothing.

Tilting his head from side to side, William listened for the shaking sound of kibbles tumbling from the box to his bowl. But the only sound he heard was the clicking of heels coming down the hall. Another neighbor appeared. She wasn't hollering or waving anything.

"Meow," cried William. He marched his front paws up and down, and walked by the stranger pressing his dark, thick coat against her shins. He pointed his nose in the air and parted his lips ever so slightly before chirping a soft "meow." The stranger bent down and scratched William under his chin and cooed in a sweet voice, but she didn't open the apartment door or bring him dinner. Instead she picked him up, carried him down the hall, opened a glass door and put him out into the night.

William stared through the door watching the woman's back get smaller and smaller as she walked down the long corridor. He nested in the soft mulch beneath one of the azalea bushes that lined the building's entrance-way, tucked his front paws underneath his body and bowed his head. But he just couldn't rest with an empty belly. He squirmed and turned until, finally, he wore himself out and drifted off into a light slumber.

Morning came quickly. William opened his eyes and blinked into the rising sun. He uncurled his body, pushed himself up and stretched his front paws, while pointing his hind quarters into the air. Then he sat very still, cautiously watching the morning rush.

Several people came out of the building, but not Sarah or her mother. William couldn't wait any longer. He had to find food.

He roamed down the walkway. "Vrooom! Whoosh!" the passing cars roared as they turned out of the parking lot. William ran away from the traffic and dove into a pile of soft autumn leaves.

He batted at a silently falling, red leaf and crouched low in the pile. Then he opened his eyes very, very wide and wiggled his rump. Suddenly, with great force, he pounced. The top blanket of crunchy leaves scattered. William rolled over and twisted, rubbing his back against the sun-warmed leaves. But he was quickly distracted—he smelled food.

William sniffed at the air and ran toward the scent. He stopped at a large green trash bin. The square opening was high, but William was able to reach the edge of the dumpster with one giant leap. He teetered some before gaining a firm grip on the rusty edges of the metal bin.

With another jump he landed on the floor of the dark box. His long whiskers served as feelers and guided him over the mounds of trash to an open bag. He pawed at it until he found several cans with scrapings of tuna fish and dog food—he licked them spotless. William's nose wrinkled and his whiskers twitched.

He made his way over piles of paper and plastic bags, bottles, and cans. The jagged rim of an opened can sliced his right, front pad. He stepped back and hissed. Then he raised the paw and gave it a quick lick before hooking his sharp claws on a piece of stale bread that covered several meaty chicken bones. He cleaned the bones, then ate the hard bread.

Just as he was taking his last bite, complete darkness crowded the opening of the bin above. William looked up just as he was hit on the head with a heavy plastic trash bag. He stumbled over another bag before regaining his balance, and carefully climbed over more broken bottles and empty cans until he was standing on top of the highest pile of rubbish. William crouched low and sprung to the ledge of the box, then down to the pavement.

He sat in another heap of newly raked leaves and bathed. His sandpaper-like tongue stroked his front paw over and over again. When the cut on his pad was no longer bleeding, he leaned back on his haunches and used both paws to wipe his face.

A familiar smell interrupted William's bath. He scrunched his nose and sniffed—a cat was nearby. William looked around. A chain-link fence separated the apartment complex from a neighborhood of houses with yards. And there, on the other side of the fence, was a small gray and white tiger cat.

William, favoring his cut paw, awkwardly pranced over to the fence and climbed up. He gazed at the cat from his perch atop the railing then jumped to the ground. Cautiously, he walked toward the cat. She stared at him. William kept walking until he was just a tails length from her nose.

She arched her back, fixed her emerald eyes on William, and gave a low, hoarse growl. Then she opened her mouth wide and hissed!

William set his ears forward and held his tail straight; slowly and silently he approached the cat.

She flattened her ears, and with a deliberate side-step, she circled William and continued to growl.

William trilled softly, and graciously bowed his head.

Just then the door of one of the houses opened. "Get! Go away!" The woman ran toward William, her hands wildly grabbing at the air. "Leave my Tigger alone," she yelled.

William made a mad dash and didn't look back until he was safely standing on the other side of the fence.

The woman picked up the tiger cat. "There, there Tiggie. My poor baby," she said carrying the tabby inside the house.

William plopped to the ground and sprawled out on his side. He perked his ears. The chirping sound was coming from a cricket rubbing its wings together. William crouched low to the pavement and crept toward the cricket. He sat up tall, casting a shadow over it.

Carefully, he covered the cricket with his paw. When William lifted his pad the cricket jumped away. William took another step and repeated his move. He kept his pad on the cricket's shell a little longer this time, but when he lifted his paw—the cricket hopped off the sidewalk and disappeared into the dew covered grass.

William walked over to the familiar azalea bush and bedded down for the night. But again he couldn't sleep. He got up several times and prowled around the building. He sniffed at several wrappers that littered the common ground. Then he returned to the bush and waited there until the whining brakes of the school bus screeched from several blocks away. He got back up, stretched his front paws, and pulled at the damp grass with razor-like claws.

"Hey, you ugly cat!" William turned toward the voice and felt the sting in his abdomen of a swiftly tossed stone. "Bulls-eye!"

"You nailed it good. My turn."

William bolted. He ran toward the sewer pipe. In the past he had amused himself by chasing mice in the sewer that ran below the street. Now the tunnel was his only protection. "Ping!" Another rock hit the pavement. William ducked into an opening at the edge of the street and escaped from the rock-wielding boys.

William stood perfectly still while his eyes adjusted to the dark. His heart raced. Finally, when the pain from the rock gave way to the ache in his belly, William crawled through the pipe making his way to the opening in front of the neighborhood store. From the street-level opening he watched the people go in and out of the market. The briny smell of fresh fish was more than he could bear. So he dug his claws into the pavement and pulled himself up onto the walk—only to be spotted by a labrador retriever. The dog gagged and coughed as he struggled to get toward William, despite his owner's firm hold on the long leash. Quickly, William retreated into the pipe. When the dog poked his nose through the opening, William gave it a good swipe.

He peered out of the tunnel again. There were other people and other dogs right in front of the store's automatic entry doors. It would be impossible to get into the store without being stampeded.

William slunk back into the pipe without his fish dinner. He continued on the same track under the street until he saw the next wedge of light marking an exit.

This was the farthest William had ever ventured from Sarah's building. But the constant emptiness in the pit of his stomach drove him past the small stores, apartment complexes and houses in search of food. He stopped at a tiny puddle and lapped at the dirty water. His tongue rubbed against the asphalt.

Then he heard a familiar noise off in the distance. It was laughter, a friendly Sarah-like sound. He set out in the direction of the voices and saw several big, yellow buses parked next to the curb. They were identical to the one that picked up Sarah. He quickened his pace.

William found the voices. There were children jumping ropes, climbing bars and running after one another. Some of the children were throwing balls back and forth.

Suddenly William felt someone standing very close. He froze— and the tiny muscles in his ears twitched. The warm breath of a stranger ruffled William's fur. He turned his head ever so slightly and

saw a boy. The boy was staring at him. William quickly surveyed the open space and dashed under one of the buses.

He crouched behind a rear tire and watched. The boy walked slowly, not like the children running and laughing in the yard. "I won't hurt you," he told William as he walked toward the bus. He lifted his sneakered feet gently with each step, and came so close to the bus it looked as if he might rub up against it. Instead, he crossed his legs and sat down on the pavement. William flattened his ears level with his head and hunched over his fore paws, ready to dart. He fixed his stare on the boy's cast down eyes.

Something rustled. William saw the boy's hand reach into a brown paper bag. The smell of food was coming from it. The boy unwrapped a sandwich, ripped off a piece and stretched his hand toward William. "You look like you could use a meal. Take it." William didn't budge.

The boy reached over and placed the piece of sandwich near a tire but not completely under the bus. William couldn't get the food from where he was hiding. He stayed perfectly still except for the rhythmic flickering of the very tip of his tail, and watched the boy wrap up the rest of the sandwich.

A deafening bell broke William's concentration. The children on the playground fell into several lines, and the boy put the wrapped sandwich back into the bag. "See ya," he said softly. Slowly, the boy pushed himself up from the pavement and headed toward the school.

William continued to watch the boy until he faded in with the rest of the children. Then he lunged from behind the tire, grabbed the scrap of sandwich and retreated back to his spot and hurriedly gulped down the food. The turkey and bread did not fill William's stomach, but it calmed the emptiness. Soon the playground was completely still; he left his hiding place and continued on his search for food.

William retraced his steps and crawled back into the sewer pipe. The steady sound of water trickling was interrupted by the sound of scampering feet. The muscles in his ears jerked. He quickened his pace and the echoing got louder. With his eyes fully adjusted to the blackness, he saw the creature responsible for the noise. It was a rat.

William crouched low to the ground. The shallow pool of water doused his dirty, white belly. He swished his tail and prepared to pounce. But just as William made his move the rat turned and raced along the wall of the pipe. William skidded smack into the concrete. He shook his head and looked around, but the rat had disappeared. A dim ray of light shone ahead; William headed toward the next opening in the pipe, and crept out.

The autumn air was chilling. William shivered. He shook off his damp coat and ran toward the apartment building.

The door was propped open, so he hurried in, and ran down the hall. When he got to Sarah's door, he was surprised that it, too, was open. A cardboard box served as a door stop. He walked inside.

Everything was different. The furniture was different, and there were new boxes all around—but there was no sign of Sarah. The smell of ammonia burned William's nose, and his whiskers twitched. He walked in and around the maze of boxes and metal furniture, and rubbed up against a carton, nudging his chin on its corner. Just as he leapt onto a box in the living room, a man came in the door with yet another box.

The man set it down in the middle of the floor, looked up and immediately spotted William.

"Meow."

"Well, hello there, kitty," the man said lifting William off the carton. He gently carried William out into the hallway and told him to "Go on home."

William held his head high and pointed his tail straight up and marched back in through the open door. "Oh no, you can't stay here," said the man as he lifted William. This time the stranger carried William down the hall and out the front door.

William tilted his head and stared at the open entrance. He didn't move until the man, carrying another box, headed back down the hall and into the apartment. William followed the same path. "Hey, didn't I tell you, no cats in the house," the man said with a stern voice.

This time when he took William out of the apartment, he closed the door behind him. William struggled to get free but the man tightened his grip and carried him to the main entrance. He placed William outside and closed that door, too.

The street lamps were lit. Few people were out in the brisk evening air, so William walked around the grounds without being threatened. A noise was coming form the direction of the dumpster—a deep, vibrating sound. Cautiously, William walked toward it. The ground shook. William slid beneath some thick evergreen branches and watched the huge truck, with long metal arms, lift the bin into the air. When the truck rolled away, William raced to the dumpster and jumped to the ledge of the heavy, metal box. He pushed his head through the plastic flap—nothing. Smells of rotten food lingered in the box, stray papers and a couple of clear, plastic newspaper bags clung to its sides, but the dumpster was empty.

William jumped down to the pavement. He ran to the fence, leaped over it, and set out in a new direction to look for food. After passing just a few houses, he picked up a wonderfully delicious smell.

He looked about and saw a bowl of cat meal sitting on a back porch. Without hesitation William ran up to the food and began eating. Half way into his feast he heard a deep growl—then a very loud hiss. He turned around and saw an enormous yellow tabby shaking his hind quarters preparing to pounce. William meowed, but the big cat would not back off. He jumped on William with great force. The weight of the tom knocked the wind out of William, and he rolled and tumbled with his attacker, unable to do much to defend himself.

Finally, William got away and stumbled toward the fence. The tabby's claw had scratched his left eye. His face was marred by several bleeding gashes, and the point on top of his left ear was sliced jaggedly in two. He tried to climb the fence but didn't have the energy to make it to the top. The yellow tabby had not followed him so William sat down leaning against the fence and tried to catch his breath. He kept his injured eye closed. Slowly, he licked his front paw and brushed it over his face.

A droplet of cold water plopped right on top of William's head. He looked up and immediately knew that the sudden breeze tickling his ears was a warning of coming rain. The autumn leaves danced circles with the wind, and the drops fell more frequently until a fine sheet of rain soaked everything that had been dry only minutes before.

William gathered his strength and climbed the fence. He forced his stiff joints to work together and half-heartedly ran for cover. The rain was falling harder and there were few dry places left. He crawled under the azalea bush, but the sparsely covered branches did not block out the pounding rain.

William dashed back out into the storm and crossed the parking lot, making his way to the sewer pipe. Down he went. But the drains were pouring water into the tunnel. He couldn't stay, so he dug his claws into the side of the cement pipe and pulled himself back onto the wet pavement. Then he ran under a parked car where there was still a narrow patch of asphalt that had not been dampened by the storm.

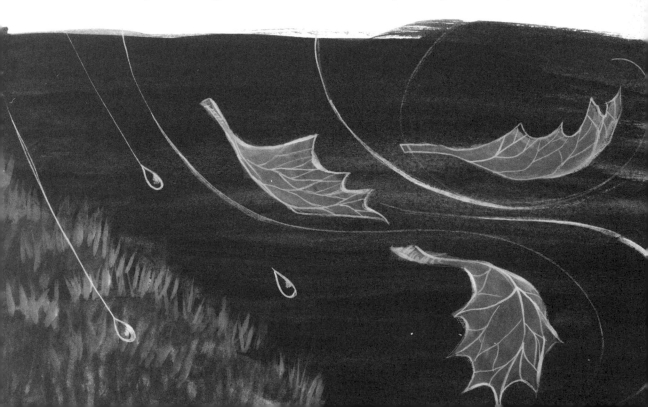

The rain stopped by sunrise. William darted from his dry place at the first boom of a car door slamming shut. He scurried back into the sewer pipe and walked through the shallow waters until he was at the exit closest to the school. There he pulled himself out and walked toward the playground. The same Sarah-like voices filled the air.

A bell sounded, and seconds later the voices faded away. William continued to walk toward the school. The grounds were now deserted. He sat down. There was no food in sight. William was tired and his injured eye needed rest.

His catnap was cut short by the return of the voices. He kept his eyes closed though, until he felt the presence of someone standing nearby. William opened his eyes and slowly turned his head. He recognized the boy who had shared the turkey sandwich with him. "Hey, you look awful," the boy said.

William cowered. The boy stood tall with his hands in the pockets of his denim jacket. "Hungry? Stay there."

William shut his tearing eye and opened his good eye wide, focusing it on the boy. The boy walked quite a distance from William before breaking into a sprint towards the building. William began to nurse his still throbbing sores. But he needed to rest. After several minutes of doctoring, the other eyelid slowly closed.

The boy's sneakers squeaked on the pavement. The noise startled William, but he did not move. He opened his good eye just a tiny bit and watched the boy bend down and kneel beside him. William pushed his ears back flat against his head and stayed very still. The area was wide open and the big yellow buses were a good distance away.

"It's okay," the boy said. Holding a brown paper bag, like the one from before, he reached inside and pulled out his lunch. The boy peeled the cellophane paper away from a sandwich.

He leaned back on his heels, removed the top piece of bread, and set the turkey and second slice of bread down on top of the smoothed-out cellophane in front of his knees.

William did not move.

"I brought this for you. Go ahead. Eat," the boy said.

William watched the boy.

"Come on," the boy whispered. "I know you're hungry."

William moved his eyes from the boy's face to the turkey that was less than a few feet away. The smell was tempting. William got up slowly. His stiff body faltered, but he became steady with the first bite of food.

"Poor ol' cat," the boy said softly. "Bet you don't have a home." William continued to eat. "You really look bad. What does the other guy look like?"

In just a few gulps the food was gone. William looked up.

"Good cat! That's better. Hey, I told my mom about you. She said, 'Malcolm, a cat is a lot of work.' My mom thinks everything is a lot of work."

Malcolm stayed seated on his heels. Feeling much stronger after his meal, William backed up a couple of feet and tried to give himself a proper bath. His sandpaper-like tongue raced over his paw, and he swept the clean paw over his face again and again. He changed paws. Then he turned his head and washed the side of his body. His sharp teeth gnawed at the mats of dirt and hair pasted together with dried blood. The back fur on his caved-in haunches began to glisten in the sun. He ignored Malcolm.

"Hey cat, recess is almost over. What do you say, want to be friends?" Malcolm wiggled closer to William and extended his hand.

William stopped his bath, stood on all fours and arched his back.

But he relaxed almost immediately as Malcolm reached his fingers
under William's chin. Gently, Malcolm scratched the skin beneath the
dirty, white fur. William leaned into the massage. When Malcolm
shifted his weight William became frightened and quickly moved
away. He didn't go far, just far enough to observe Malcolm from a
safe distance.

"Sorry. Hey, c'mon. Let's be friends." Malcolm sat down on the
pavement and crossed his legs. He stretched his hand out toward
William. William stared.

Finally, with a cautious step, William walked toward Malcolm but avoided his touch. When he was so close he could feel Malcolm's breath on his coat, he sped up and walked right past him. He turned around, retraced his steps and came just a few paces shy of rubbing up against Malcolm's back. He followed the same pattern several times.

"C'mon, cat. I gotta get back to school. Hey, you gonna be here at three o'clock?"

William stopped his parade and watched Malcolm talk. He glanced at the extended hand. He inched closer. Then he leaned his chin toward the welcoming fingers and nudged at Malcolm's hand. His muscles relaxed as he bowed into the steady movement of Malcolm's fingers.

William closed his eyes and purred.